A GOLDEN BOOK • NEW YORK

Text copyright © 2011 by Tim Moore

Illustrations copyright © 2011 by Pete Whitehead

All rights reserved. Published in the United States by Golden Books, an imprint of
Random House Children's Books, a division of Random House, Inc., 1745 Broadway, New York, NY 10019.
Golden Books, A Golden Book, and the G colophon are registered trademarks of Random House, Inc.

This book is based on the song "Must Be Santa" written by Hal Moore and Bill Fredricks. Copyright © 1960 Hollis
Music. Renewed 1988 in U.S. by Intuitive Music and Woodwyn Music and administered in U.S. by Intuitive Music.

www.randomhouse.com/kids

Educators and librarians, for a variety of teaching tools,
visit us at www.randomhouse.com/teachers

Library of Congress Control Number: 2010932160

ISBN: 978-0-375-86853-5 (trade) — ISBN: 978-0-375-96853-2 (lib. bdg.)
ISBN: 978-0-375-98006-0 (ebook)

MANUFACTURED IN CHINA

10 9 8 7 6 5 4 3

First Random House Edition 2011

Must Be Santa

By Tim Moore

Based on the popular song by Hal Moore and Bill Fredricks

Illustrated by Pete Whitehead

Who's got a beard
that's long and white?

Santa's got a beard
that's long and white!

Who comes around
on a special night?

Santa comes around
on a special night!

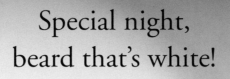

Special night,
beard that's white!

Must be Santa!

Must be Santa!

Must be Santa!

Santa Claus!

Who wears boots
and a suit of red?

Santa wears boots
and a suit of red!

Who wears a
long cap on his head?

Santa wears a
long cap on his head!

Cap on head,
   suit that's red.
Special night,
   beard that's white!

Must be Santa!

Must be Santa!

Must be Santa!

Santa Claus!

Who's got a big
red cherry nose?

Santa's got a big
red cherry nose!

Who laughs this way?—
Ho, ho, ho!

Santa laughs this way—
Ho, ho, ho!

Ho, ho, ho!

Cherry nose.

Cap on head,

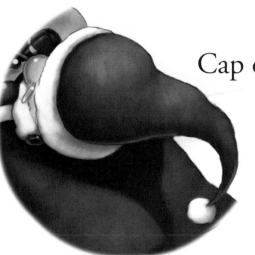

suit that's red.

Special night,

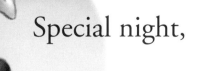

beard
that's white!

Must be Santa!
Must be Santa!
Must be Santa!
Santa Claus!

Who very soon
will come our way?

Santa
very
soon
will
come
our
way!

Eight little reindeer
pull his sleigh.

Santa's little reindeer
pull his sleigh!

Dasher!

Donner!

Comet!

Blitzen!

Prancer!

Cupid!

Vixen!

Dancer!

Reindeer sleigh,
come our way.
Ho, ho, ho!
Cherry nose.
Cap on head,
suit that's red.
Special night,
beard that's white!

Must be Santa! Must be Santa!
Must be Santa!
Santa Claus!